ZORA, THE STORY KEEPER

written by **Ebony Joy Wilkins**

illustrated by **Dare Coulter**

Kokila

WHEN I GROW UP, I want to be just like my aunt Bea. She is the best storyteller I know.

Aunt Bea used to teach acting classes, and sometimes she dresses up in costume and uses funny voices when she tells her stories. She says everyone has a story worth telling.

My page is near the end of the book. I think about what Aunt Bea will read about me—maybe that I like making snow angels and running races with my cousins at our family reunions.

Each day after school, Aunt Bea reads to me from the
pages of our family book while Mom and Dad are working.

I learned that Grandma Jean used to coach a swimming team. Aunt Bea pulls on a swim cap and swings a whistle around her finger when she tells that story.

We also read that Grandpa Tom preached sermons in our neighborhood church in Chicago, so Aunt Bea wears a purple robe and dabs her forehead with a white cloth.

Sometimes I dress up, too, and
her kitchen becomes our stage.

Maybe she'll read that I want to play tennis like Serena and Venus, I plan to be a veterinarian, and I hope to visit all 54 countries in Africa one day.

"What's written on my page?" I ask Aunt Bea daily.

"I'll give you a hint, Zora," she says excitedly. "It's something we both love to do."

Sometimes there's only a name, date, or city written in our book, so we have to piece together the stories. Aunt Bea says I have a good memory and the gift of gab, the only two things you need to be a good storyteller.

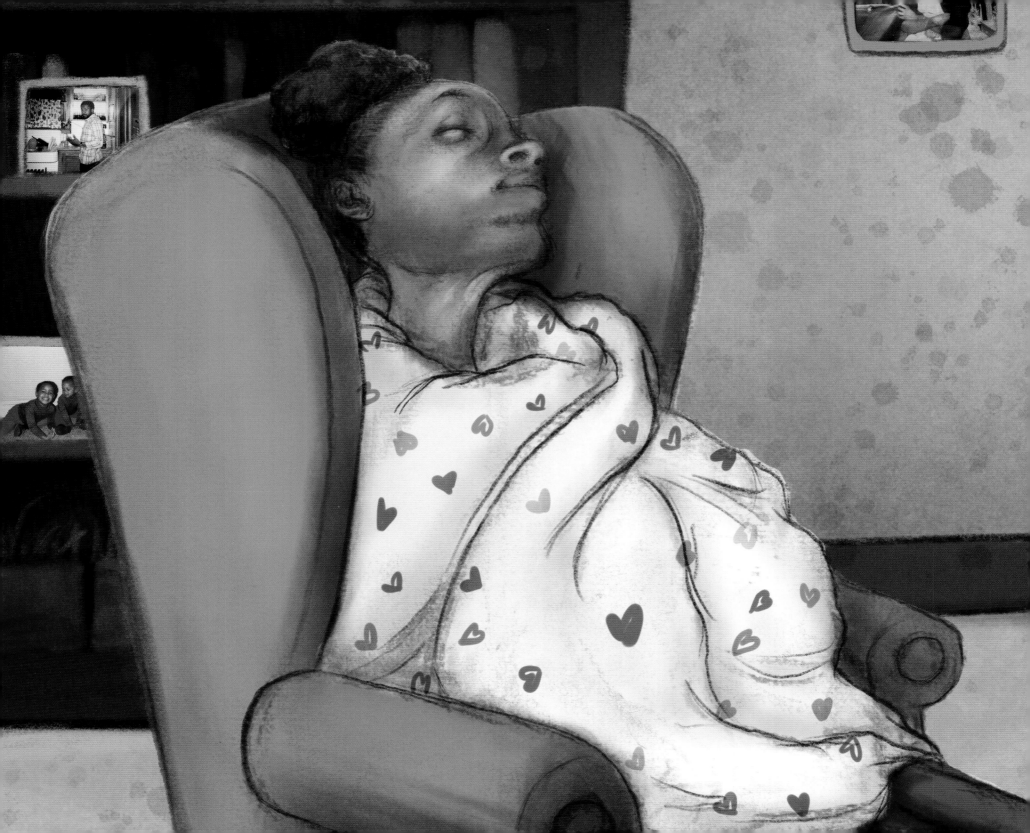

One day, the family book is open to Uncle Ted's page, but Aunt Bea isn't in costume yet. She's resting. She opens her eyes when I touch her shoulder and tells me I'll need to help her today.

I bring over my toy soldiers and line them up on the arm of her chair. Aunt Bea smiles as I shout orders to my platoon just like Uncle Ted did. He was a fighter pilot in World War II. When one of his men fell to the ground during battle, Uncle Ted risked his life and flew him to safety.

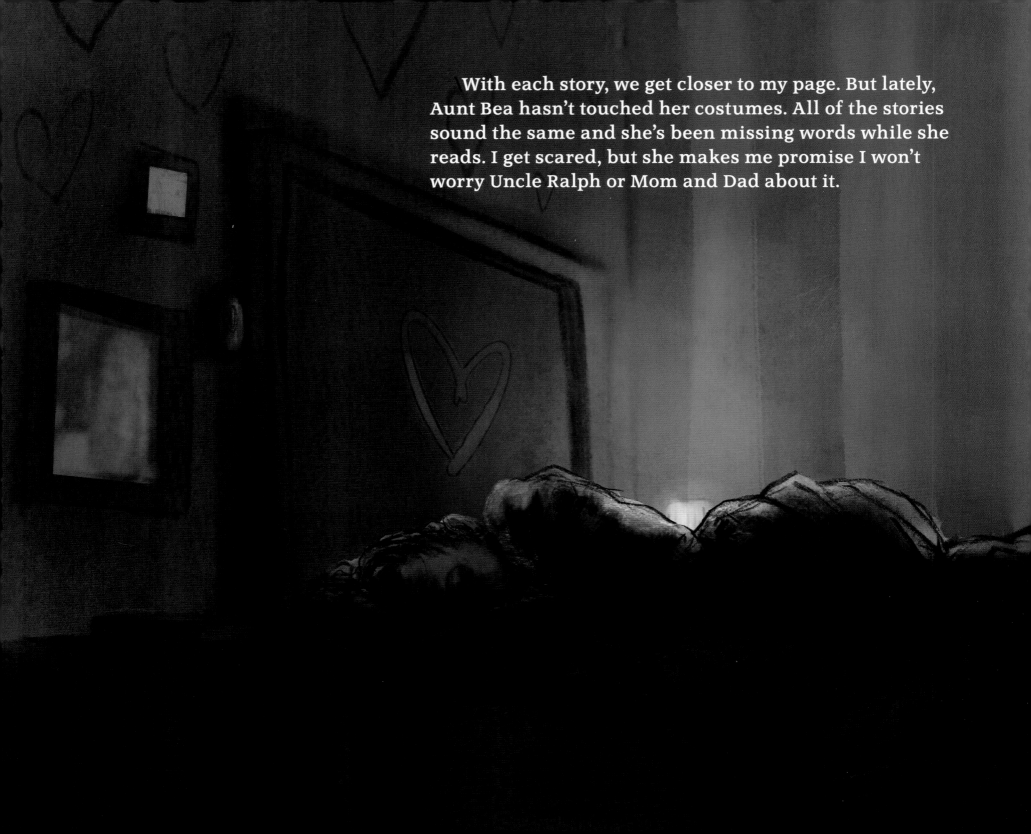

With each story, we get closer to my page. But lately, Aunt Bea hasn't touched her costumes. All of the stories sound the same and she's been missing words while she reads. I get scared, but she makes me promise I won't worry Uncle Ralph or Mom and Dad about it.

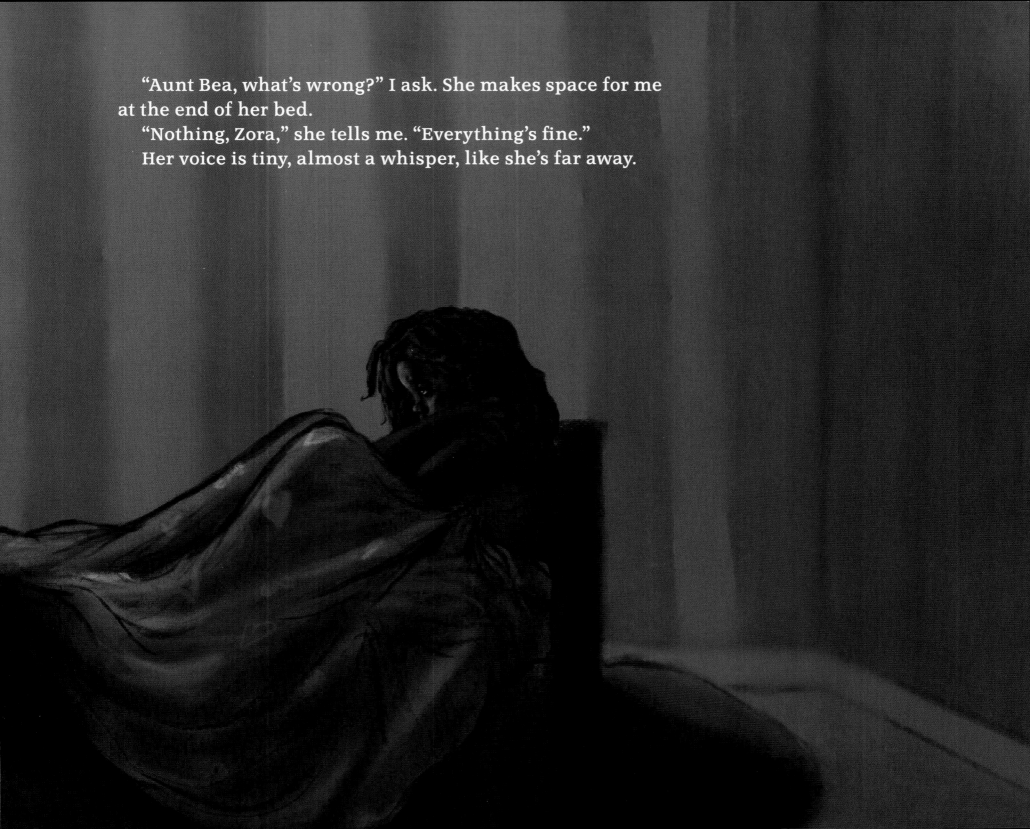

"Aunt Bea, what's wrong?" I ask. She makes space for me at the end of her bed.

"Nothing, Zora," she tells me. "Everything's fine."

Her voice is tiny, almost a whisper, like she's far away.

Uncle Ralph says the doctors want to keep an eye on Aunt Bea's levels, and I am to tidy up the house while they're away. I dust her favorite books first, the ones written by Zora Neale Hurston. When I get to our family book, I leave it near Aunt Bea's pillow for when she comes home.

Uncle Ralph comes back, but Aunt Bea isn't with him. He drops down on the sofa and wipes a tear from his eye. Miles Davis is singing about love in the background.

When the doctors say I can visit, I brush Aunt Bea's hair and tell her a story about Cousin Cheryl's sewing shop in the Bronx, where she made the most glamorous beaded gowns with matching headpieces. Women came from all five boroughs to buy from Cheryl's Sew & Design.

Aunt Bea smiles proudly. I tell her stories until the nurses say it's time to let her rest. I hug her tight, but Aunt Bea feels soft like one of my dolls. I kiss her forehead and tuck her blanket under her chin.

Aunt Bea isn't coming home.

There are no stories for a few days.

Mom sets my Sunday dress on the bed. I slip it on, pull my locs up into a high bun, and step into my cowgirl boots. Aunt Bea and Uncle Ralph's place is full of family. Everyone knows to bring a dish—and a photo and a story for our family book. Aunt Bea's stories were much better than the ones I hear today.

I sink deep into Aunt Bea's armchair. That's where Uncle Ralph finds me after everyone goes home.

"Your aunt wanted you to have this," he says.

There's a silver bow and a card with my name written on top. The smooth leather feels familiar, like home. The pages smell like Aunt Bea's pound cake. I open the cover slowly, and he hands me an envelope full of photos. On the backside of each one, I find names and dates. He says I'm to add them to the book.

I turn to the last page. My story is there, just like Aunt Bea said it would be. There's a message next to my name: *Zora, the Story Keeper*. I make space for Uncle Ralph to sit.

As I add the photos to Aunt Bea's page,
I start to piece her story together.

Aunt Bea

To Mom and Dad: Thank you for always
keeping our history and stories alive.
—E. J. W.

To all the people I have ever loved, and who have loved
me back. And if I've never met you I hope you know, in the words
of the Davids, you are beloved, and that excludes no one!
To my mom and sisters, for being the story of my life,
and to dear wonderful Rubin and everything you've put into
making sure that I get to tell stories to the world with my art.
—D. C.

Kokila
An imprint of Penguin Random House LLC, New York

First published in the United States of America by Kokila, an imprint of Penguin Random House LLC, 2023

Text copyright © 2023 by Ebony Joy Wilkins
Illustrations copyright © 2023 by Dare Coulter

Penguin supports copyright. Copyright fuels creativity, encourages diverse voices, promotes free speech, and creates a vibrant culture.
Thank you for buying an authorized edition of this book and for complying with copyright laws by not reproducing, scanning,
or distributing any part of it in any form without permission. You are supporting writers and allowing
Penguin to continue to publish books for every reader.

Kokila & colophon are registered trademarks of Penguin Random House LLC.
The Penguin colophon is a registered trademark of Penguin Books Limited.

Visit us online at penguinrandomhouse.com.

Library of Congress Cataloging-in-Publication Data is available.

Manufactured in China

ISBN 9781984816917

1 3 5 7 9 10 8 6 4 2
TOPL

This book was edited by Joanna Cárdenas and designed by Jasmin Rubero.
The production was supervised by Tabitha Dulla, Nicole Kiser, Ariela Rudy Zaltzman, and Caitlin Taylor.

Text set in Accolade.

The illustrations were created almost entirely on an iPad, using Procreate with
brushes from the Gouache MaxPack and a 6B brush from LeUyen Pham (thank you!).
Some illustrations started with charcoal on paper, and the painting of Uncle Ralph
on the couch is mostly an acrylic painting. Final edits were done in Photoshop. The
photographs are pictures from both Dare Coulter's and Dr. Ebony Joy Wilkins's lives.
The art for this book is a love letter.